Reeya Rai and the King's Treasure

written by Anita Nahta Amin

illustrated by Farimah Khavarinezhad and Marta Dorado

STONE ARCH BOOKS
a capstone imprint

Published by Stone Arch Books, an imprint of Capstone.
1710 Roe Crest Drive
North Mankato, Minnesota 56003
capstonepub.com

Library of Congress Cataloging-in-Publication Data
Names: Amin, Anita Nahta, author.
Title: Reeya Rai and the king's treasure / Anita Nahta Amin.
Description: North Mankato, Minnesota : Stone Arch Books, an imprint of Capstone, [2024]
Series: Reeya Rai: adventurous inventor | Audience: Ages 8-11. | Audience: Grades 4-6.
Summary: In Rajasthan with her archaeologist parents Reeya Rai finds an ancient stepwell, with an underwater door bearing a mysterious symbol which may be the key to a legendary treasure—if she can come up with an invention and find it before her rival Elsie Acker.
Identifiers: LCCN 2023014143 (print) | LCCN 2023014144 (ebook)
ISBN 9781669033981 (hardcover) | ISBN 9781669034087 (paperback)
ISBN 9781669034049 (pdf) | ISBN 9781669034094 (epub)
Subjects: LCSH: Treasure troves—Juvenile fiction. | Archaeologists —Juvenile fiction. | Inventions—Juvenile fiction. | Adventure stories. Rajasthan (India)—Antiquities—Juvenile fiction. | CYAC: Buried treasure—Fiction. | Archaeologists—Fiction. | Inventions—Fiction. Adventure and adventurers—Fiction. | Rajasthan (India)—Fiction. LCGFT: Action and adventure fiction. | Novels.
Classification: LCC PZ7.1.A4986 Re 2024 (print) | LCC PZ7.1.A4986 (ebook) | DDC 813.6 [Fic]—dc23/eng/20230509
LC record available at https://lccn.loc.gov/2023014143
LC ebook record available at https://lccn.loc.gov/2023014144

Credits
Aaron Sautter, editor; Elyse White, designer;
Whitney Schaefer, production specialist

Image Credits
Shutterstock: highviews, 7 (bottom left), reddees, 7 (bottom right), xamnesiacx84, 65

Design Elements
Shutterstock: Hulinska Yevheniia, inspired-fiona, Lera Efremova, LeshaBu, Pattern_Repeat, Redberry, Tartila, Timmy Tayn, Veronique G, Witthawas Suknantee

Printed and bound in the USA. PO 5626

Table of Contents

Hiya, it's Reeya!

I'm Reeya Rai! I was born in the United States, but my Hindu family is originally from India. My parents are archaeologists. I love to travel along on their adventures all around the world!

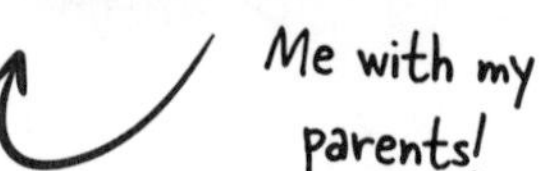

I also love to invent things that help my parents with their cool discoveries. I invented Tink! He's pretty useful to have around.

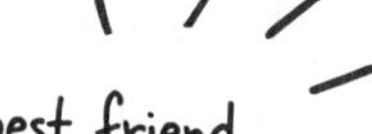

This is my best friend, Finlay Finnegan, and his parents!

Finlay is a whiz with computer code and electronics. He helped me program Tink! His parents are archaeologists, too. They work with my Dad and Mom.

Elsie and her dad, Dr. Acker

Elsie is definitely NOT a friend. She's bossy and spoiled. Her dad, Dr. Acker, is a rival of my parents. He's jealous of their work and often shows up whenever my parents make a big discovery.

Hindu Culture

Hindu homes are often filled with large families. Grandparents, parents, siblings, uncles, aunts, and children often share a home. The home may be passed down through many generations. Elders, not just a parent's siblings, are called "auntie" or "uncle" to show respect.

Hindus remove their shoes before entering a house or temple. The streets outside are considered filthy with germs and dirt. Shoes are removed to prevent tracking dirt and germs inside.

Beef is forbidden in a strict Hindu meal. Many Hindus don't eat meat at all. Hindus believe cows are holy because they give milk, which can sustain life. They do not hurt or kill cows. Cows are often allowed to roam freely in towns and villages.

Karma is one law of Hinduism. Hindus believe that if you are good, good will come to you. If you do something bad, you will receive something bad in return.

Dharma is the law that tells Hindus how they should behave. It teaches them to be kind, patient, and honest, among other virtues.

Words to Know

chai (CHAH-ee)—tea

han (HAHN)—yes

katli (KUHT-lee)—a diamond-shaped sweet fudge made of nuts such as almonds or cashews

pranam (prah-NAHM)—a greeting that shows respect; it often involves pressing the palms of the hands together and sometimes bowing and touching the other person's feet

purana (poo-RAH-nuh)—old

sari (SAH-ree)—a long fabric that wraps around to form a sort of dress worn by women and girls in India

katli

sari

Chapter 1
Digging for Treasure

Looking across the sand dunes, Reeya Rai saw sandstone turrets that stood tall against the mango-colored sky. The ancient ruins looked like a fabled, long-lost city.

Reeya buttoned her jacket to block the winter chill and climbed out of the car. This was her first trip to Rajasthan, India, her grandparents' homeland. She and her parents were traveling with her best friend, Finlay, and his parents. Reeya couldn't wait to get out and explore.

"Let's go find some treasure!" Dad grinned.

Reeya and Finlay exchanged amused looks. Their parents were archaeologists. Sometimes, treasure meant gold or jewels. But mostly, it meant broken bits of pottery, scraps of fabric, or spice dust. They loved learning about history.

As they walked toward their new dig site, Dad pointed to the remains of a palace. It was more than 2,000 years old. They decided to peek inside. But it was empty.

"Where did the king's treasure go?" Reeya asked.

"It was probably stolen over the years," Mom said.

"Or someone moved it," Dad said. "Like the Chain of Justice. You would've liked that invention, Reeya."

Reeya's ears perked up at the word "invention." Under her arm was her most valued possession. It was a notebook filled with notes and drawings of inventions she had thought up. She loved how inventions could change the world. She wanted to help people too.

Reeya asked, "What is the Chain of Justice?"

Dad explained. "Long ago, a king invented it for his people. It was an eighty-foot chain with sixty bells made of gold. If someone pulled the chain and rang the bells, they could speak with the king. But according to legend, the king was overthrown and exiled. Then his chain was hidden."

The story about the chain sparked Reeya's imagination. She wondered if she could invent something to track it down. She wrote down "Chain of Justice" in her notebook.

"That's amazing!" Reeya exclaimed. "Do you think we'll find it?"

"You never know," Mom smiled. "Sometimes, artifacts hide in plain sight. People see them every day and don't realize how important they are."

The group continued on to their dig site.

Workers there were dividing the ground into sections with string. The sections would help keep track of where they found any artifacts.

"*Pranam*," Mom and Dad said to the workers in Hindi, an Indian language. They pressed their palms together with their fingers pointed up under their chins. Finlay's parents copied the gestures too.

"Come on kids," Mom said, waving them over. "You can help dig over here."

A couple hours later, they hadn't found any artifacts. Dad stood up with a sigh and dusted sand off his pants. "That's enough for today."

As their car turned onto a sandy alley, Reeya admired the village's tall houses. Designs were carved into the open doors. Murals were painted on the walls, inside and out.

They stopped in front of a house. Several aunties and uncles were with a boy about Reeya's age. Reeya recognized her cousin from their video chats.

"Chotubhai!" Reeya shouted. She leaped out of the car and hugged him. She introduced Finlay.

"Hello!" Chotubhai said, smiling and stepping back shyly.

Mom reminded Reeya to greet her elder relatives. Reeya bent down and touched their feet, one person at a time, to show respect.

"Pranam," the elders replied in Hindi. Then everyone slipped off their shoes and went inside. The family members all lived together. Reeya, Finlay, and their parents would stay there too.

Chotubhai showed Reeya and Finlay to a bedroom to unpack. In a bag he discovered Tink, the toy robot Reeya and Finlay had built together. Reeya had first gathered all the gears, wheels, and other needed parts. Then, after they put Tink together, Finlay programmed him to follow their commands. The friends played with Tink and explored the house all afternoon.

That night, Reeya wriggled on her lumpy bed. It was made from strips of old *saris* that were sewn together and stuffed with cotton. Reeya thought about her Dad's disappointment at the dig site. She wanted to help him find some artifacts or treasure—maybe even the Chain of Justice! But how? Suddenly, her eyes snapped open. She knew just what to do. She would invent a Treasure Tracker!

Chapter 2
The Well

The next morning Reeya sat at the breakfast table. She stared at a page in her notebook. She had written "Treasure Tracker" at the top of the page. But she was stuck. What would a Treasure Tracker look like? How would it work? She had no idea. She sighed with frustration and munched on a *katli*. The diamond-shaped piece of almond fudge was covered with edible silver foil.

Dad wandered in, reading a map.

"What are you doing, Dad?" Reeya asked.

"I'm studying our digging site. We're planning to explore this ancient stepwell." He held the map upright and pointed to a circular area on it.

"What is a stepwell?" Reeya asked.

Dad explained. "It's a type of Indian invention. With most wells, people have to lower a pail to fetch water. But with a stepwell, people can walk down to the water. Then they can bathe, do laundry, wash animals, or do other things that need water."

Reeya imagined bathing in a deep stepwell. She thought it would be scary to not be able to touch the bottom.

Chotubhai finished his mango and turned to Reeya and Finlay. "Do you know cricket?"

"I caught one once, but my mom wouldn't let me keep it," Finlay said.

Chotubhai shook his head. "Not that kind of cricket. I mean the sport. Come, I'll show you!" He went and got a ball and bat from his bedroom.

As the friends headed to the door, Reeya heard a commotion outside. Chotubhai's family had left their front door open. People in their village often did that so neighbors could visit any time.

A familiar voice was shouting. "But I want to go to the pool and take videos!"

"Oh no. Not her . . ." Finlay grimaced as Elsie Acker appeared at the door.

Reeya frowned. Elsie was always rude and bossy, and often irritated her.

Elsie and her father, Dr. Acker, strolled into Chotubhai's home. Dr. Acker was an archaeologist from another museum.

"Good morning," Dr. Acker said. "My helpers informed me you were here. We're staying in the boarding house down the street." His greedy eyes raked over the room and lingered on Dad's map.

"Welcome," Dad politely said, rolling up the map and putting it away.

Chotubhai's mom offered tea and sweets, but Dr. Acker waved her away dismissively. He turned back to Dad and said, "I'm curious about what you've found so far. My site is close to yours."

Meanwhile, Elsie pushed her way past Reeya. As she did, she cried out, "Watch it! You almost made me drop my new camera!"

Before Reeya could respond, Elsie said, "My camera can take videos underwater. Look!"

Elsie turned the camera on, then dunked it in a water pot. Then she fished it out of the water and showed off the video to everyone.

An underwater camera! Reeya had never used one before. "Can I try?"

Elsie held her camera away. "No, you might break it."

"Er . . . we were just leaving to play cricket. Do you want to join us?" Chotubhai invited Elsie before Reeya could stop him. She hoped Elsie would say no.

Elsie narrowed her eyes at them. After a moment, she shrugged. "Sure, I guess."

As they hiked to Chotubhai's favorite spot, they nudged cows out of the way. Soon, the homes faded away to mud huts and wide fields of mustard plants. Beyond the plants, women were walking with pots on their heads.

"We're here," Chotubhai said when they reached an open clearing. He explained how to play cricket. It was sort of like baseball.

"I'll go first!" Elsie demanded, grabbing the bat.

Chotubhai pitched Elsie the ball. *Whack!* Elsie struck the ball. It sailed high over the plants.

"Wow, look how far I hit it!" Elsie exclaimed.

"I'll get it," Reeya said when Elsie didn't move. Reeya pushed through the tall, flowering mustard plants, looking everywhere for the ball. But she couldn't find it.

On the other side of the field, Reeya found some women who were washing clothes and bathing a goat. They sat on stone steps around a murky pool of water. Reeya wondered if the ball had landed in the water. She climbed down the steps but couldn't see the bottom of the pool.

She didn't feel like searching for the ball, so decided to leave. But as she climbed back up the steps, she realized something.

"Is this a stepwell?" Reeya wondered aloud.

The structure was triangular, and the steps looked old. The sandstone was worn, crumbling, and mossy in some spots.

Reeya pointed to the well. "Old?" she asked the lady with the goat.

The woman looked confused.

Reeya knew only a few words of Hindi. She struggled to find the right word. "*Purana*?"

The woman said, "*Han*."

Reeya grew excited. She had found an old stepwell that could be thousands of years old. She couldn't wait to tell her parents about finding an ancient treasure hiding in plain sight!

Chapter 3
The Sari Rope

Reeya was excited to tell her parents about the stepwell. But what if it wasn't actually ancient or important enough? Her parents were busy. She didn't want to waste their time. She needed to find out more about the well first. She wondered how deep it was. Did the steps go all the way down? And what might be at the bottom?

"What's taking so long?" Elsie shouted, making her way across the field with Finlay and Chotubhai.

Reeya didn't want Elsie to see the well. She might tell her father. Then Dr. Acker might take credit for finding it!

Reeya hurried back and grabbed Finlay and Chotubhai by their arms. "I can't find the ball anywhere. Let's go home," she said, gently tugging them along.

"But I didn't get a turn to bat," Finlay complained.

"What about my ball?" Chotubhai frowned.

Elsie hung back, her eyes narrowing. "The ball has to be here somewhere."

"N-no! I'm tired." Reeya faked a yawn and opened her eyes wide to let the boys know to play along.

"Whaa . . . oh!" Finlay looked confused but followed Reeya's lead. "I'm tired too."

"Yes, as am I," Chotubhai said, stretching out his arms. "Let's go."

Elsie frowned but followed them, since she didn't know the way home. When they reached her house, she ran inside with a "Hmph!" and slammed the door behind her.

With Elsie gone, Reeya darted up the alley, through the open gate, across the sandy courtyard, and up the steps into her cousin's house.

"What's going on?" Finlay panted, catching up.

"Yes, why the rush?" Chotubhai asked, breathing heavily.

Reeya told them what she had found in the mustard field.

"Oh, yes. That has been there for years," Chotubhai said. "But for how many years? I don't know."

"Do you know what this means?" Finlay cried. "Our parents could become famous! *We* could become famous!"

"We don't know for sure that it's ancient," Reeya reminded him. "Or even what's under all that water. We need to find out how deep it is. Then we can figure out how to check the rest of the well. But how do we measure the depth?"

"My ruler won't work," Chotubhai said. "It's too short."

"A laser measuring tape?" Finlay said. "But we don't have one."

"What about a long rope?" Reeya asked after seeing her bed through her open doorway. "We can make it out of old saris."

Chotubhai went to ask his mom for old saris. He brought back a small stack of faded cotton and silk fabrics. Some still shimmered with stray gold threads and sequins. "I told my mom you need them for a big invention," Chotubhai told Reeya.

Reeya and the boys cut the saris into strips and tied them together to make a long rope.

Chotubhai measured the length of the rope with his ruler. "It's forty feet long. Do you think it's enough?"

"There's only one way to find out," Reeya replied.

Carrying the rope between them and keeping an eye out for Elsie, they hurried to the stepwell.

"Okay, let's see how deep the water is," Reeya said. She looked around and found a large rock. She tied the rope around the rock and slowly lowered it into the well. Chotubhai held the other end of the rope. The rock kept going deeper and deeper. Reeya wondered when it would stop.

"Wow, this is deep," Finlay said.

"That's all of the rope," Chotubhai finally said.

"So it's at least forty feet deep!" Reeya said excitedly.

Chotubhai walked over to speak with a woman collecting water nearby. When he came back, he said, "She says no one has ever seen the bottom of this well. It has never dried out. It always stays full with rainwater and groundwater."

"I wonder how we can see the bottom?" Reeya thought for a moment. They could scoop out the water with a pail or try to pump it out. But that would take forever. Plus, people in the village needed the water to survive.

If only she knew how to scuba dive, then she could dive to the bottom of the well and see what was down there. But she didn't know anything about diving. However, . . .

"I have an idea!" Reeya said.

Chapter 4
Building a Treasure Tracker

Back at Chotubhai's house, Reeya watched for her parents to get back from work. "We have to tell you something!" she said excitedly when they finally arrived.

"We found a stepwell—" Finlay started.

"And it's quite old!" Chotubhai interrupted.

"We're going to build a Treasure Tracker to look under the water," Reeya said. She explained her idea to explore the well. "It will be a submersible machine that dives down and takes videos."

Dad frowned. "I've never seen a triangular stepwell. Are you sure it's a stepwell?"

Reeya shrugged. "It has steps and goes down to the water. What else would it be?"

"I like your idea, Reeya. But you must be careful not to pollute the well," Mom said. "People depend on the water."

"We'll be careful," Reeya promised. "We won't leave the Tracker in the well."

"You had an interesting day," Dad said. "We did too. We also found something. It might be a key!"

"A key—" Chotubhai started.

"—to what?" Finlay interrupted.

"What does it look like?" Reeya asked excitedly.

"We don't know what it unlocks yet, but it looks like this." Dad drew a picture of the key in Reeya's notebook. It had four prongs and a handle that looked like a wheel.

Reeya and the boys raced up to the rooftop to plan the Treasure Tracker. Together, they thought about what functions the tracker would need and wrote them down in Reeya's notebook.

Tracker requirements: move forward, sink forty feet, record video, keep the inside circuits dry, come back to the surface.

As they talked about it, the tracker grew clearer in Reeya's mind. She imagined a device that looked like an underwater airplane. She drew a diagram and realized it would need several parts to work.

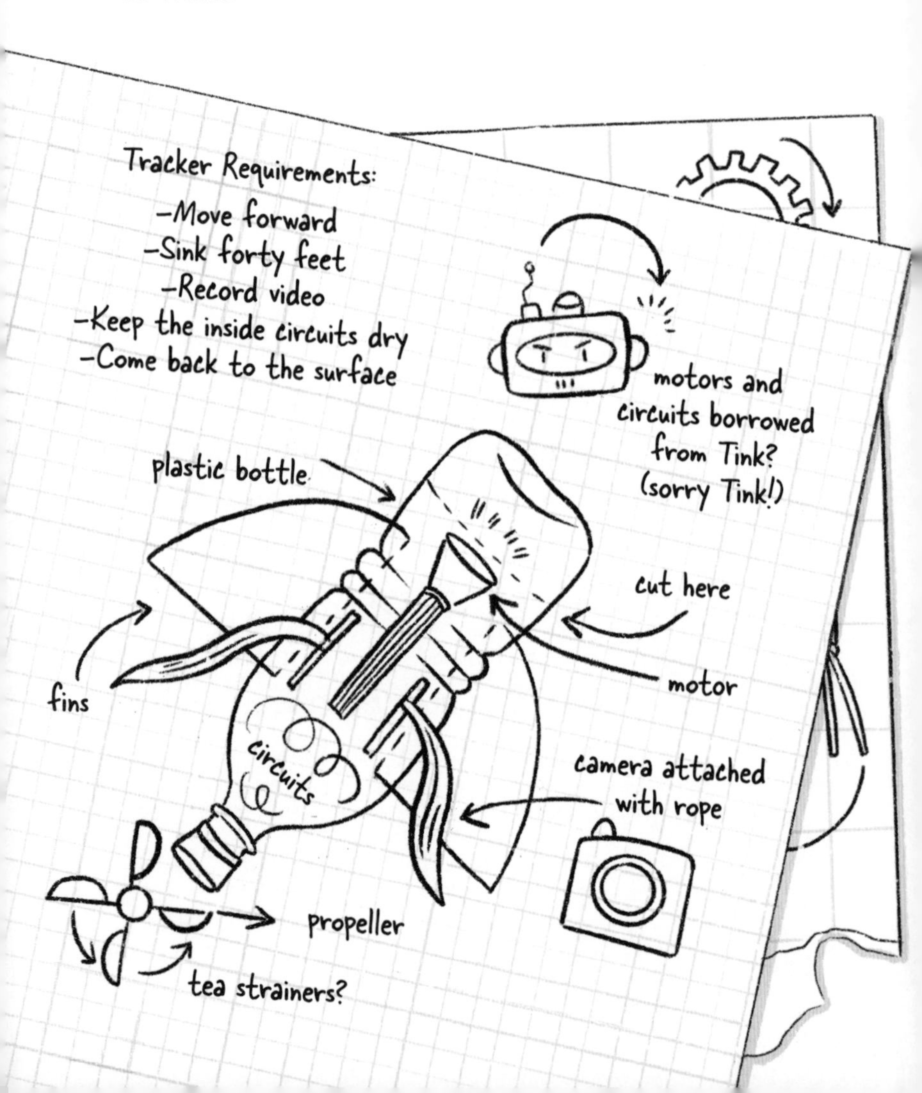

Unfortunately, she could think of only one way to get the parts. "We'll have to take Tink apart," Reeya said, breaking the bad news to Finlay. She told him which parts they needed.

Finlay's face fell. "But it took us forever to build Tink."

"I know," Reeya said sadly. She didn't want to do it either. "But we'll rebuild him, I promise. We'll need his remote control to steer the sub too."

Finlay shuffled down the stairs to get the parts.

"The sub will need a light too if the well is dark," Chotubhai said, thinking out loud. He left to get some battery-operated lights for the tracker.

Meanwhile, Reeya poked through some items she had picked up earlier. She knew the sub would need to be waterproof and strong enough to handle the water pressure. As it sank deeper, the heavy weight of the water could break it.

"This might work," Reeya said, pulling out a large plastic bottle. She used scissors to cut off the top of the bottle to fit parts inside. Then she cut out plastic fins and glued them to the sides of the bottle. This would be the body of the sub.

Next, she needed to make a propeller to push the sub through the water. She headed to the kitchen downstairs to look for something that could work as a propeller. Some small tea strainers caught her eye.

If I join them together, they might make a good propeller, Reeya thought.

She saw a lit candle on the counter too. She remembered that wax repels water. She could scrape out the soft candle wax and wrap it around any exposed parts to make them waterproof.

Chotubhai's mom blew out the candle and motioned for Reeya to go ahead and take it and the strainers. "Thank you," Reeya said.

Reeya headed back to the roof, where the boys were waiting. Parts and lights lay on the ground next to them. The three friends quickly got to work. They stripped, twisted, hooked, and plugged in wires to connect the parts. Reeya carefully slid the tangled parts and wires into the bottle. Then she fit the propeller onto the motor shaft.

"Let's test it," Reeya said. She pushed the power button. But nothing happened.

"Let me check it." Finlay closely checked each wire. "Aha! This might be the problem." He changed two wires that were hooked up the wrong way. "See if it works now."

They all held their breath as Reeya pressed the power button. The motor whirred and *whoosh!* The propeller spun around and around.

"Yes! It's working!" Reeya cheered.

She then prepared the spot where the camera would be mounted. She cut two slits in the bottle. Then she threaded part of the sari rope through the slits. She would use the sections of rope hanging out to tie the camera to the bottle. She dabbed glue over the slits to keep the bottle waterproof.

Chotubhai put the lights inside the bottle. Then Reeya smoothed wax over the exposed part of the motor. She sealed the chamber with a layer of plastic and glue. Now, she just needed to mount a camera under the bottle.

"There's just one problem," Finlay said. "We don't have a waterproof camera."

Reeya sighed. She knew this moment would come, and she didn't want to face it. "No. But we know somebody who does."

"Elsie will never let us borrow it," Finlay said, frowning.

"We have to find a way," Reeya said. She knew it was almost impossible that Elsie would agree to let them use it. But they needed her special camera.

Chapter 5
A Trade

The next morning, as the friends bounced down bumpy dirt roads in a motorized tuk-tuk cab, they still didn't have a plan. They had stopped at Elsie's house, but she had already left with her father.

Chotubhai shrugged. "Here we share everything. If we ask Elsie, do you think she would not help?"

"You don't know her like we do," Finlay said. "She won't help." He had already given up.

"There must be a way to make a deal with her," Reeya said.

At the dig site, the parents were already hard at work. Reeya's mom sifted dirt from a pail. Meanwhile, Dad was labeling a bag of artifacts.

Just then, Reeya spotted Elsie nearby roaming around with her camera.

Reeya pushed up her glasses and approached Elsie. "Hi! Playing cricket was fun yesterday."

Elsie narrowed her eyes. "Yeah, until you left."

Reeya tittered nervously. "Sorry, I really needed to get home. So, have you taken more videos with your camera?"

"Yes! See?" Elsie turned on the camera and showed Reeya another video.

"Wow," Reeya said. "Your camera takes great videos. Do you think I could borrow it for a little while? It's for an important project."

"What? No!" Elsie hugged her camera close.

"Please? I promise to take really good care of it," Reeya pleaded. "I'll do your digging for you."

Elsie narrowed her eyes. "My dad doesn't let me dig. Why do you want my camera?"

"I can't tell you," Reeya said.

"Then I can't give it to you." Elsie turned on her heel and stomped away.

"Now what do we do?" Reeya sighed as Finlay and Chotubhai joined her.

"I don't want to say it, but I told you so," Finlay said.

A while later, a young chaiwala passed out clay cups of sweet *chai*. Dad bought boxes of sweets for everyone to share. Reeya helped herself to a katli. As she ate her snack, she noticed that Elsie was watching them from a distance.

Reeya had a thought. Maybe Elsie would trade her camera for katli! Reeya held up the box of sweets and called out to Elsie. "Do you want one?"

Elsie made a beeline for the sweets. "Are you having a party?"

"No, just break time." Reeya held out the box and Elsie picked a katli. She closed her eyes as she ate one after another. "You're lucky. My dad never gets these."

"What if we trade?" Reeya asked. "You can have all of my katli for a week if you let me use your camera until tomorrow."

"Tomorrow? That's a long time!" Elsie looked from the sweets to her camera, appearing torn. "Wait, I can take the videos for you."

Reeya shook her head. "Sorry, that won't work. You only get my katli if you let me use the camera on my own."

"Okay . . ." Elsie said slowly. "But then I want your katli for a month instead."

Reeya frowned. A *month*! This deal wasn't going well. But there was no choice. She had to have that camera.

"Umm . . . okay, agreed," Reeya said, holding out her hand.

Elsie smirked and handed over the camera. She walked away with the rest of Reeya's sweets.

"I don't believe it," Finlay said when Reeya returned with the camera.

"Let's go finish the Tracker, before Elsie changes her mind!" Reeya said.

* * *

Back at Chotubhai's house, Reeya tied the camera to the bottle. "We need to test it in water. But it can't be too deep in case it breaks apart."

"My school has a pool," Chotubhai said.

They walked to Chotubhai's school, where monkeys scrambled onto the roof of an open-walled classroom. The students were away for winter break, but the headmaster was working there. He greeted them and waved them on.

At the pool, Reeya placed the Treasure Tracker in the water and turned it on. As it began to sink below the surface, the propeller spun. Finlay used the remote control to make the tracker move around.

"It works!" Reeya cried with relief, high-fiving Finlay and Chotubhai.

But there was one problem. The sub wouldn't rise back up. "It's too heavy," Reeya said. "But we can use the rope to pull it out. We'll just need to make it longer so the tracker can move around inside the well."

The rest of the day, Reeya could only think about one thing. What would the Treasure Tracker find tomorrow?

Chapter 6
The Door

The next morning, Reeya peeked out of the gate in front of Chotubhai's home. She scanned the alley and looked toward Elsie's boarding house. Nearby, a man pulled a cart of sizzling spiced nuts. Some women strolled by with their anklets and bangles clinking. But there was no sign of Elsie.

"It's all clear," Reeya said, motioning for Finlay and Chotubhai to follow.

Carrying the Treasure Tracker and their gear, the three friends had just passed Elsie's place when a milk taxi turned down the alley and beeped. Suddenly people poured out of their homes with pots and pans. They clamored for the milkman to ladle milk for them from a giant vat hooked to the back of his taxi.

"Are you sure this is milk? Why does it taste funny?" Reeya heard a familiar voice ask.

Reeya froze and looked back. It was Elsie! And she had seen them! Reeya gave Elsie a quick wave and walked faster. "She saw us!" she hissed.

"She's following us!" Finlay cried, looking back.

"Do not worry!" Chotubhai said, speeding up. "We will lose her. I know some shortcuts."

He turned down another alley that smelled of marigold flowers that hung on doorways. They ran through smoke that hung in the air from frying crackers. Soon, they blended into the crowd at a bazaar.

"Ew! That's disgusting!" Elsie cried. Reeya looked back to see Elsie frantically scraping her feet in the sand. Elsie had stepped in a pile of cow poop!

The three friends darted through an open-wall sari shop and out the back door. After a few more turns, they passed a boy walking with a goat.

"I think we lost her!" Reeya cheered as she looked back. "Good job, Chotubhai!"

Chotubhai pointed to the mustard fields ahead. "And look, here we are!"

No one else was at the stepwell as they set up the tracker. Finlay set up his laptop to watch the video.

"The signal is weak," Finlay said, "but hopefully we'll see some of the video."

Reeya lowered the sub into the well and turned everything on. It raced along the water, slowly going down until it was out of sight. Reeya held her breath. Would it break apart as it went deeper?

The friends' eyes grew wide as they watched the camera's livestream on the computer screen. Hundreds of steps crisscrossed down to various floors that held various columns and arches. All of it repeated over and over again like a maze.

Suddenly, the tracker's lights flickered and the image blurred. "We're losing the signal," Finlay frowned.

"Wait, what is *that*?" Reeya asked as the image flashed into focus for a moment. They had reached the bottom of the stepwell! There, in a dim corner far away, an outline was etched into the wall.

"It looks like a door. I think there's a lock on it."

"I wonder why?" Chotubhai asked.

"Maybe there's treasure behind it!" Finlay said.

"Do you see a key lying anywhere?" Reeya asked. They searched the video but couldn't find anything that looked like a key.

Then Reeya noticed there was a pattern on the door. It looked like a wheel. The shape somehow seemed familiar. And where was the key? Without it, how would they see what was behind the door? Plus, even if they had a key, how would they open a door that deep underwater?

Chapter 7
Proof for the Parents

Reeya, Finlay, and Chotubhai pulled together on the rope to bring their invention to the surface. The wet rope was slick and heavy. It dripped everywhere as they hurried back home.

When Reeya and the boys burst through the door, their families were enjoying teatime. The friends all talked over each other as they tried to share their discovery.

"One at a time please!" Dad said, laughing.

"We found something important. Look!" Reeya played the video for him.

As they watched the video, Dad's eyes suddenly grew wide. "Wait, stop!" he cried. "Zoom in on that door."

Reeya zoomed in on the wheel above the door.

Dad gasped. "That looks like—"

"The key!" Reeya interrupted, realizing why the wheel seemed so familiar. She opened her notebook to Dad's picture of the key. She compared the key handle and the wheel design on the door. They looked the same. "Do you think this is the key that will open this door?"

"I don't know," Dad said. "But it's a good possibility."

"It would be nice to explore the stepwell and see what's behind the door," Mom said. "My uncle works for the government. Maybe he can get us a permit to study this well."

"How will you study it if it's full of water?" Reeya asked. "Are you going to move the water?"

"No," Mom said. "We can't move the water. People will get upset. They don't have water pipes in their homes here. The well is the only source of water for many in the village."

"There isn't a place to move the water to either," Dad said. "And we can't just dump it. Water is precious. We can't waste it."

"But we're not underwater archaeologists," Finlay's dad said. "We don't have the right equipment to explore underwater."

"Diving might be our only option," Finlay's mom said.

"Someone needs to dive down there," Finlay's dad agreed. "But who?"

"We don't know how to swim," Mom said about herself and Dad.

"I've never dived before, but I could take lessons," Finlay's mom offered.

"Me too," Finlay's dad said.

Dad frowned. "Maybe. But that would take time away from the dig site. We still have a lot of work to do there."

"We could hire a diver," Mom said. "But they might tell Dr. Acker. Then he might try to take over. He could take any artifacts to his museum in Britain. Or worse, he might try to sell them."

Reeya frowned. The thought of diving deep into the well was frightening. But she didn't want to lose the chance to learn more about the stepwell, or to see what was behind the door.

"I, uh . . . I could learn to scuba dive."

Finlay and Chotubhai gaped at her.

Mom refused. "No, Reeya. It's much too deep. And you're too young."

"I know ten-year-olds who scuba dive!" Reeya protested.

"What about Ajay or Asha?" Dad asked about friends he knew. "They're underwater archaeologists. One of them might be able to fly here and help."

"That's a great idea," Mom said.

"But I can dive," Reeya insisted. "I want to help."

Mom shook her head. "It's not safe."

"Well, can I take lessons at least?" Reeya asked.

"We know someone who can teach her," Chotubhai's mom said. "He can probably meet with her tomorrow."

Mom mulled this over. "Hmmm . . . lessons with an experienced teacher might be okay."

"Thank you!" Reeya hugged Mom.

Later that evening, Reeya went to record the results of the Treasure Tracker's dive down the well. She was too excited to sleep. She would learn everything she could about diving. Then she would find a way to convince her parents to let her dive in the well.

Chapter 8
Learning to Dive

The next morning, before going to her first scuba lesson, Reeya trudged to Elsie's house. "Thanks for letting me borrow the camera," Reeya said. She handed it to Elsie along with her katli.

Elsie cradled her camera like a long-lost pet. As she walked away, she tried to find Reeya's video in the camera's memory. But Reeya had already deleted it.

Chotubhai met Reeya back at his house, and they walked to the pool together. Reeya felt excited but nervous at the same time.

"Don't worry," Chotubhai said. "Coach Sharma is the best."

When they got there, a short man with a mustache stood by the pool. He smiled and waved his hand to join him.

"Hello, I'm Coach Sharma. I'll be your scuba diving coach." He spoke in English.

Coach Sharma helped Reeya put on a diving vest. As he adjusted it, he explained the different parts. The vest had some hoses sticking out of it. A mouthpiece was attached to one hose. An air tank was attached to the back of the vest. It was so heavy that Reeya wondered how she would stand, much less dive.

"What is the refrigerator thing again?" Reeya asked. She was already confused!

Coach corrected her. "You mean the regulator. It's the mouthpiece. You breathe air from it through your mouth. The vest is called a buoyancy control device. It lets you control how deep you dive. If you let air out of it, you'll descend. Pump air in and you rise."

Whoosh! Hiss! The vest deflated and inflated with air as Coach pulled a string and pushed a button.

Reeya tried to remember what he did. She also learned how to read the diving gauges and compass. She learned hand signals. She didn't really feel ready yet, but Coach handed her a mask. She took off her glasses and followed him into the shallow end of the pool.

She clamped her mouth around the mouthpiece, and they dove under the water.

Ffsshhh! Her breathing sounded like a rattlesnake. *Glub, glub.* Bubbles streamed up as she exhaled.

She kicked her fins and followed her coach to the deep end. Reeya was amazed to feel weightless like an astronaut!

As the lessons continued for the next few days, Reeya needed less and less help with her gear. Finally, Coach said, "You're a natural! Next time, we'll try a lake. It's about two hours from here, so we'll need to take a train."

Reeya was happy with her progress. But when the time came to go diving in the lake, she had second thoughts. A lake was a lot deeper than a pool!

* * *

"Just follow my lead and remember your hand signals," Coach Sharma said. "I'm here with you."

Two days later, they were sitting on a boat on the lake. Her parents, Chotubhai, and Finlay were there too. Today, Coach had Reeya put on a wet suit along with her diving vest. He said it would help her stay warm in the cold water.

Reeya followed as Coach splashed into the lake. Without her glasses, everything looked blurry. Reeya flailed her arms and legs, and she drew quick shallow breaths. Suddenly she couldn't remember how to use her equipment!

A school of large carp swam around her. Reeya had never seen anything like it. Her amazement at the fish helped her relax. Coach used hand signals to ask if she was okay.

Reeya flashed the "Okay" signal to Coach, and they dove deeper. Ten feet, twenty feet, thirty feet . . . They glided over plants, swam by an old sunken rowboat, and checked out an underwater cave. Then they headed back up.

When they finally burst through the water's surface, Reeya wanted to dive again. The next few lessons sped by. Before long, Reeya made it down to forty feet! She wanted to go deeper, but Coach said it wasn't safe for someone her age.

At the end of the last session, he said, "Great job! You've finished scuba school!"

Everyone on the boat cheered.

"But remember," Coach Sharma warned. "Stay safe. Always be sure to dive with a buddy."

A dive buddy? The only diver Reeya knew was Coach. How would she dive in the stepwell without someone else there?

That evening at dinner time, Mom waved a piece of paper. "The government approved our permit!" she said. "We can officially study the stepwell, but only for a short time."

"That's great! But I have bad news," Dad said. "Ajay and Asha can't come. They're stuck on other projects."

The room fell silent. Without Dad's friends to help, how would they explore the stepwell?

"I can do it," Reeya said.

Mom shook her head. "Not by yourself. You heard Coach Sharma. You need a dive buddy."

"I know," Reeya said. "I was thinking . . . what if he comes with me? I know we can trust him."

The parents looked at each other. "That might be a good idea," Dad said. "I'll ask him."

* * *

The next day, Dad announced, "I spoke with Coach Sharma. He said he'll dive down the stepwell with Reeya tomorrow."

Reeya's heart jumped with joy. She couldn't believe it! But nobody had ever dived in that well before. What if it was dangerous? What if the key didn't work? What if the door didn't open? Too many things could still go wrong.

Chapter 9
Down the Well

The next afternoon, Reeya and Coach Sharma sat on the slick steps of the stepwell. The winter sun looked like a cold white ball in the sky. Smog blocked its warmth. Reeya shivered. She was cold—and nervous. She checked her swimsuit pocket. The key was still there.

Coach and Reeya pulled their fins onto their feet and adjusted their diving vests.

"You can do this," Coach told Reeya, "Just remember your training." Then they plopped into the dark well water.

"We can see you on my screen, too," Finlay reminded them. "If there's a problem, just wave."

Coach Sharma had his own underwater video camera. It was tied to his wrist and linked to Finlay's computer. Reeya wished she had known about Coach's camera before she gave all her katli to Elsie.

Coach Sharma gave the signal and they dove down. Five feet, ten feet, twenty feet . . . Reeya peered through the water. Their flashlight beams danced across the sandstone pillars and hidden nooks. Hundreds of crisscrossing steps wrapped around the well.

Reeya stopped to look at a flower sculpture carved into a balcony. She ran her fingers along the carving, amazed at its beauty.

She started to feel more comfortable and descended farther. She kept going, studying the stepwell until she realized something. Coach Sharma was no longer by her side!

Where had he gone? She stopped and looked around. She couldn't find Coach. She was starting to panic when she looked up and spotted him. He was still at the flower balcony. He seemed to be struggling to free himself from it. He was stuck and needed help!

She rose as quickly as she could and saw that his air hose had snagged on the flower. She helped him untangle his air hose, and he was free. He signaled that he was okay, and they kept going.

At forty feet, Reeya glided along the walls, looking for the door. Suddenly, in a corner, she saw the wheel! Around it was the outline of a door.

Trash and dirt had collected on the well floor around the door. Reeya and Coach scraped it away with their hands. Reeya took the key out of her pocket and slid it into the lock. She wiggled and jiggled it. But it wouldn't turn.

She motioned for Coach to try. He twisted the key, but the lock wouldn't budge. It must have rusted in place. Feeling desperate, Reeya jammed the key forward and shoved it side to side one last time. Finally, the key turned!

Reeya and Coach looked at each other with wide eyes. Together they pushed the door with all their strength. It scraped the stone floor as it slowly opened. Reeya's eyes grew wider and wider, knowing they would soon see what was behind the door.

Inside, the dark room was filled with water and one other item. Their flashlight beams landed on a shiny object lying in the center of the room. It was a long golden chain holding dozens of golden bells!

Chapter 10
A King's Treasure

Reeya couldn't believe her eyes. She counted the bells. There were sixty of them! And the chain was at least eighty feet long! Was it possible? Had they just found the legendary Chain of Justice?

Reeya and Coach Sharma tried to lift the chain, but it was too heavy. Coach pointed up with his thumb. She didn't want to leave, but they would have to come back for the chain later.

When they came to the surface, everyone rushed to help them and cheered.

"You found the Chain of Justice!" Dad exclaimed. "We saw it on the computer!"

"This is the find of the century!" Mom cried.

"We were worried when Coach Sharma got stuck," Chotubhai told Reeya and Coach.

Finlay agreed. "Next time you need a headset and microphone, Reeya. We weren't sure how to get your attention."

"But it turned out okay in the end, thanks to Reeya," Coach Sharma smiled.

"I'm glad I could help," Reeya smiled. "And next time, I'll make sure I stick with my buddy."

Finlay's parents were busy congratulating Reeya when someone cleared their throat behind them. It was Dr. Acker! Elsie was with him too.

"Congratulations," Dr. Acker said. "Elsie told me she saw all of you coming over here with scuba gear. I thought you might need my help."

"Thank you," Mom said. "But we have enough help right now."

Dr. Acker gave a curt nod and left with Elsie. When they were farther away, Reeya overheard him hiss at Elsie, "Why on earth did you help the competition?"

Elsie turned and shot an angry glare at Reeya.

The next morning, Reeya woke up to the sound of the telephone ringing. She heard Mom answer it. After a few moments, Mom poked her head into the bedroom.

"I thought you'd want to know. Government officials are going to move the Chain of Justice to the national museum."

"That's great news!" Reeya replied. She was glad the chain would stay in India. Its history and future belonged to the country.

Before breakfast, she headed to Elsie's place with her katli. Elsie opened the door angrily.

"You didn't tell me you were going to use my camera to find treasure!" Elsie accused.

Reeya wanted to be fair. "No, but I'll make sure you get credit for your camera in any news about the chain."

"Hmph!" Elsie huffed, but she seemed calmer.

Later, as Reeya munched on rose petal biscuits and drank hot milk, she jotted down ideas in her notebook for future versions of the Treasure Tracker. Finally, she scrawled across the bottom of the page: Treasure Tracker version 1.0 = success!

"Now let's play cricket!" Chotubhai said. He and Finlay had just finished fixing Tink.

The boys convinced Reeya to go along, but she wasn't going without her inventions notebook. She made sure to tuck it into her pocket. Whether her inventions helped fix problems, solve mysteries, or find treasure, Reeya wanted to be a part of them all!

racker Requirements:
-Move forward
-Sink forty feet
-Record video
the inside circuits dry
e back to the surface
plastic bottle
cut here
motor
circuits
camera attached
with rope
propeller
tea strainers?

Build a Submersible!

You can make your own plastic bottle submersible, inspired by Reeya's invention! Gather some supplies and ask an adult to help you build this rubber band-powered sub.

Materials needed:

- 1 large plastic bottle, including cap
- 1 long, heavy-duty rubber band
- 1 large paper clip
- 4 plastic spoons
- 1 tack
- tape
- ruler
- pen or pencil
- scissors

What to do:

1. Straighten the paper clip in the middle. Slip one end of the rubber band onto one hooked side of the paper clip.

2. Measure mark an X at 3 inches (7.6 centimeters) from the bottom of the bottle. Ask an adult to help you cut an X in the bottle at that mark. Make the X as wide as the spoon handles. Insert the handle of a plastic spoon into one X. This will be one of the fins. Repeat this step to add a second fin on the other side of the bottle.

3. Lower the free loop of the rubber band into the bottle. Hook it around one of the spoon handles. Push the spoon handle through the hole on the other side of the bottle. Repeat with the other spoon handle so the rubber band is looped around both handles and they are held in place.

4. Ask an adult to help push the tack through the center of the bottle cap.

5. Measure and draw a dot 1.5 inches (3.8 cm) from the bottom of the handle on the third spoon. Repeat with the last spoon. Ask an adult to push the tack through each of the dots to make a hole in the spoon handles.

6. Straighten the part of the paper clip not attached to the rubber band. Thread the straight part through the hole in the bottle cap. Twist the cap back onto the bottle. Hold the end of the paper clip so it doesn't slip back into the bottle.

7. Thread the end of the paper clip through the holes in the spoon handles. Arrange the spoons so they point in opposite directions like a propeller. Tape the handles together.

8. Flatten the paper clip onto the spoon handles and tape it in place.

9. Test the propeller. Turn it ten times to wind up the rubber band inside, then let go. It should spin freely. If not, make sure the rubber band, paper clip, and propeller aren't snagged anywhere.

10. Open the cap and fill the bottle halfway with water. Lay the bottle on its side in a sink or bathtub filled with water. The water should be deep enough so the propeller doesn't touch the bottom. Wind up the propeller 30 times. Then place the sub in the water and watch it go!

More About Stepwells and India

- Stepwells were first built in India in the 200s CE. That's almost 2,000 years ago!

- The deepest stepwell is Chand Baori, built in the 800s CE in Rajasthan, India. It has 13 underground floors and is 100 feet (30.5 meters) deep with 3,500 steps. Baori is a Hindi word for stepwell. Chand Baori translates to moon (chand) stepwell (baori).

- Half of the people in India don't have enough water. They may walk for miles to fetch a pail of dirty well water for the day.

- The monsoon, or rainy season, is three months long from July to September. Most of India's rain for the year falls during this time. It helps to fill the wells and water crops.

- In the 1600s CE, King Jahangir had a Chain of Justice strung between Agra Fort and the Yamuna River in North India. The gold chain was 80 feet (24 meters) long and had 60 bells. The citizens pulled it to request a meeting with the king.

Chand Baori stepwell in Rajasthan, India

- Along with the stepwell, other inventions from ancient India include yoga, some types of surgery, and an early version of chess.

- Cricket is a popular sport in India. It is similar to baseball, and is played with a ball and a bat that looks like a paddle. Bowlers on one team throw balls to try to break two wickets. A wicket is a set of three short posts with planks across them. The batsmen try to hit the balls away from the wickets. If they hit the ball, they can try to score a run.

Talk About It

1. Sometimes artifacts are stolen or taken as trophies during times of war. They may be placed in museums or private collections in other countries. Do you think artifacts should be sent back to the countries they came from or kept where they are? Why or why not?

2. Reeya was afraid of diving at first. Have you ever been afraid of doing something risky? What did you do or could you do to help overcome your fear?

3. Have you ever had to work with someone you don't get along with very well? What are some ways that helped you work together? What can you do to help you get along better?

Write About It

1. Reeya keeps a notebook to write down her invention ideas. Can you think of any inventions that might be helpful to your school or community? Get a notebook to write down your ideas. Write out a plan to build your invention. Then test it out and write down the results.

2. Reeya learns in this story that, unlike her home in the United States, many people in India must travel to places like stepwells to get water. Imagine you are one of these people. How is their experience different from yours? Write about the challenges you might face carrying water from a stepwell back to your home.

3. Write a short story about joining an archaeological dig. Where would you travel to in the world? What might you find?

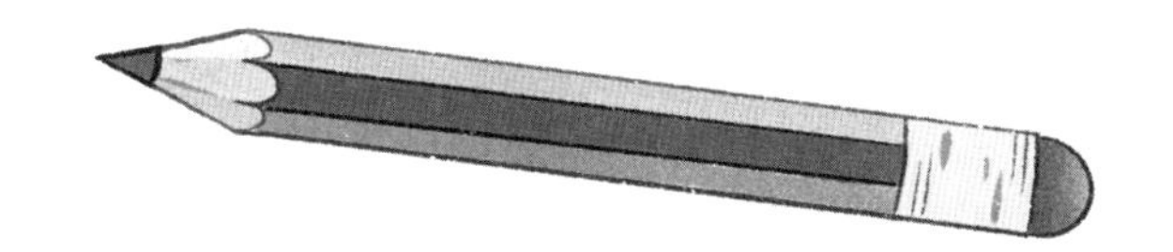

Glossary

bazaar (buh-ZAR)—a street market

chaiwala (chahy-WAH-lah)—a person who sells tea in India

exiled (EG-zahyld)—ordered to leave one's country and live somewhere else

gauge (GAYJ)—a dial or instrument used to measure something

livestream (LAHYV-streem)—to transmit or receive live video on the internet while an event is taking place

monsoon (mon-SOON)—a season of the year in some parts of the world that is known for heavy rainstorms

submersible (suhb-MUR-suh-buhl)—a small underwater craft powered by a motor

tuk-tuk (TUHK-tuhk)—a motorized three-wheeled vehicle with a small cab for passengers mounted behind the driver

turret (TUR-it)—a small tower, usually on top of another structure such as a castle or palace

Anita Nahta Amin

Anita Nahta Amin is a second generation Indian American and former information technology manager. She is the author of several fiction and nonfiction children's books. Her notebook is one of her most prized possessions, and she is always writing ideas in it.

Farimah Khavarinezhad

Farimah Khavarinezhad is a freelance illustrator currently based in Canada. She loves incorporating details into her illustrations, with warm and cozy colors. Her favorite thing about illustrating is that it is similar to magic. Illustrations bring characters and elements to life.

Marta Dorado

Marta Dorado was born in Gijón, Spain, and raised in a nearby village. She later moved to Pamplona to attend university, where she still lives. Her childhood was surrounded by nature and close to the sea, which has strongly influenced her work.

Hiya, it's Reeya!

Read up on all my adventures with my family and friends.

Hurry, before Elsie or her Dad grabs them first!